MOOG-MOOG,
Space Barber

by MARK TEAGUE

SCHOLASTIC INC.

New York   Toronto   London   Auckland   Sydney

ON the last day of summer,
Elmo Freem's mother took him
to the barbershop.
"I want you to look nice
for your first day of school," she said.
The barber, Mr. Kleeg,
was a kind old man, but the haircut
he gave Elmo was not very good.
In fact, it was awful.
Even Elmo's baseball cap
couldn't cover the problem.

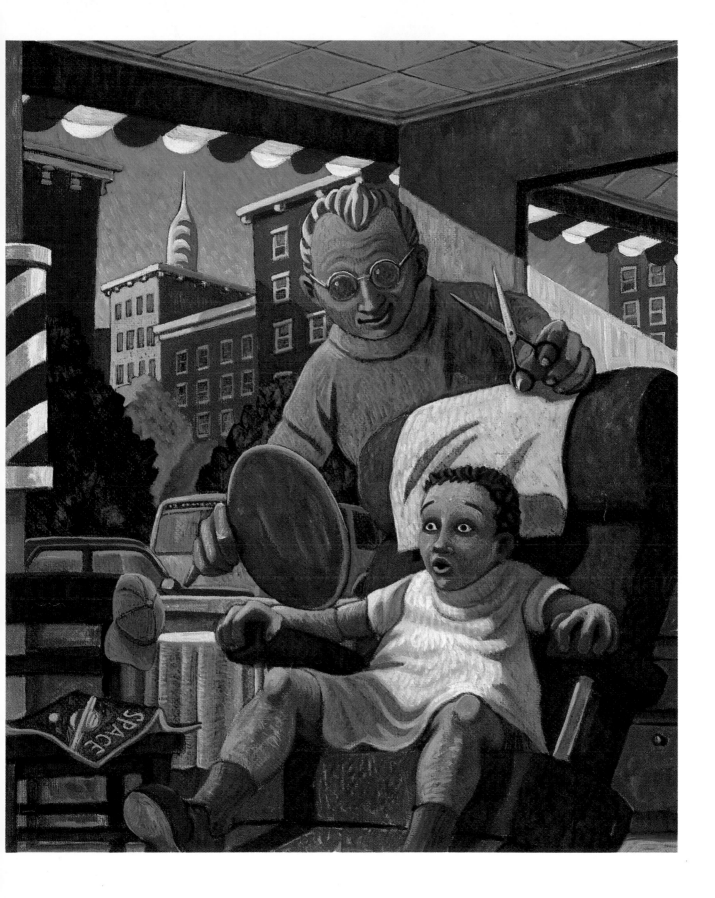

Back home, Elmo tried combing his hair in various ways, but it was no use. He could imagine what the kids at school would say when they saw him.

With the help of his cat, Leon, he found a stocking cap in one of his dresser drawers. He'd never liked the cap much, even in winter, but now it seemed like the only solution to his problem. Elmo put the cap on, then sat down on his bed and watched the clock tick away the rest of his summer vacation. He dreaded the next morning, when Buford Snark would come by to walk with him to school. Buford was his best friend, but even so, he was sure to make fun of such a silly haircut. Elmo couldn't stop the morning from coming, but at least he could put it off for a while. "I will stay up all night," he thought.

After his parents went to bed, Elmo and Leon snuck into the living room and turned on the television. They watched a movie called *Big Slimy Things From Outer Space*.

In the movie, large, green, pointy-headed monsters land in a place called Mellville Corners and begin tearing up the entire town. Things are pretty bad for the townspeople until someone invents a special X-ray gun to use against the space monsters.

"If only things were really that simple," thought Elmo.

During a commercial
Elmo and Leon went to the kitchen
to get a snack.
They were horrified
to find a couple of space monsters
standing by their refrigerator,
drinking milk straight
from the carton.

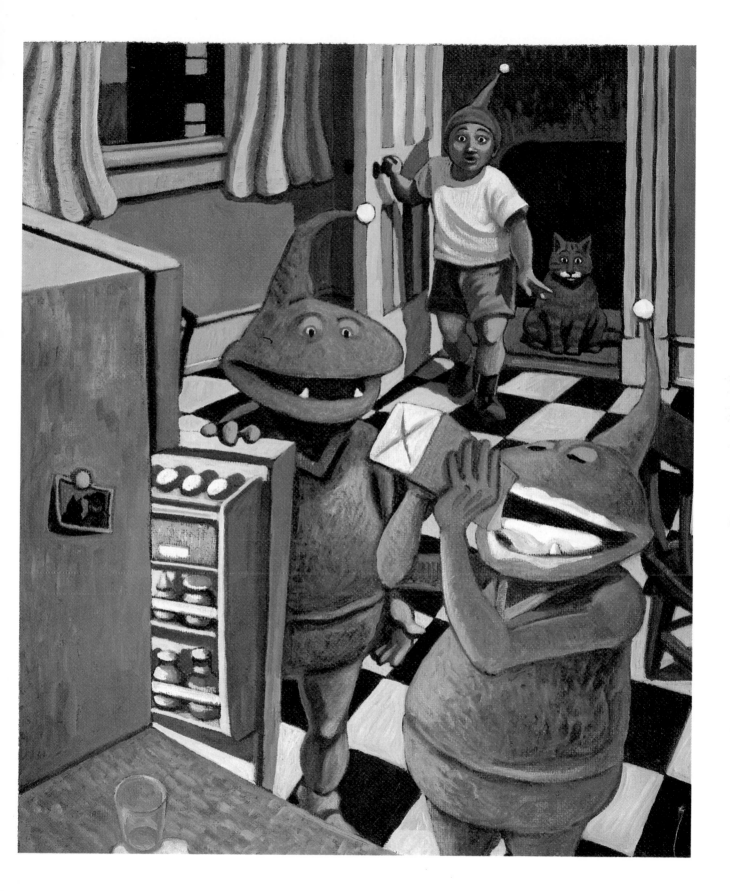

The monsters never explained why they were in Elmo's kitchen, and Elmo never got a chance to ask. For when the creatures saw his cap, they welcomed the boy as one of their own. "Goomba!" they cried as they covered his face with great, slimy monster kisses.

"Wait!" said Elmo, and he quickly explained that he was not a monster at all, just a boy with a bad haircut. To prove it, he took off his cap.

"Why, you are an earthling," said one of the space creatures.

"I see what you mean about that haircut," said the other.

"What's worse," said Elmo sadly, "is that tomorrow is the first day of school."

"Oh, dear," they said. Not even monsters look forward to the first day of school.

For a while everyone was quiet. Except for Leon, they were all thinking about Elmo's problem. Leon was still thinking about the snack he had come to the kitchen for in the first place.

Finally one of the monsters spoke up. "Moog-Moog," he said.

"Of course!" said the other monster.

"What?" said Elmo.

"Moog-Moog is the finest barber in the universe," the monster explained. "If he can't solve your problem, nobody can. But come now, we must hurry."

The next thing Elmo knew, he and Leon were being carried out the kitchen window.

The monsters' spaceship was parked
on the roof of Elmo's apartment building.
Elmo and Leon were placed in the backseat
while the creatures hopped in front.
"Hold on!" said the driver,
and with a roar the ship flew off,
over the city and into space.

As they sped along, Elmo and Leon stared out through the ship's glass dome. Elmo recognized several planets from a book he had at home. Then somewhere near Saturn they made a left turn and headed off into a strange part of space. They flew past stars and planets and comets and moons, until finally they came to a small, green planet dotted with clouds.

"Here we are," said the monsters. "The planet Moogie."

The spaceship flew lower and lower, until it nearly skimmed the tops of trees and houses. The planet was very beautiful, and in some ways, almost like Earth. It reminded Elmo of Mellville Corners in the movie. Then the monsters pointed out a wonderful palace standing high on top of a hill. "There it is," they said. "Moog's barbershop."

Elmo was impressed. "That's some barbershop," he said as the ship touched down.

Moog-Moog was as wonderful as his shop.
He had beautiful pointed teeth
and a head of hair that changed colors
as he moved.

"Oh, dear," he said when he looked at Elmo,
and he called for his assistants
to bring him his tools. "Here is a challenge
worthy of the Great Moog!"

The barber set to work
with scissors and clippers, electric buzzers
and pruning shears.
Then he tried crinklers and curlers,
hair stretchers and even
his X-ray blowgun.
A crowd began to gather.
Elmo was embarrassed
by all the attention.
"It's just a haircut," he said.

Moog worked for hours and hours, and threw all of his skills into the problem, but it was no use.

"Alas," he said finally, "the Great Moog has been defeated."

Elmo felt sorry for the barber. "Really," he said, "I think it looks much better." It didn't, but saying so seemed to help.

"Do you really think so?" asked Moog, as the crowd cheered.

"Oh, yes," said Elmo, "it's very nice."

It was a long ride home. Elmo hoped that his adventure had at least caused him to miss the first day of school, but he had no such luck. By some mystery of space travel they arrived back at the apartment just moments after they had left. In fact, *Big Slimy Things From Outer Space* was still playing in the living room. The monsters stayed to watch the ending. They agreed that the movie was pretty good.

Before they left
they wished Elmo luck
on his first day at school.
"Wear the cap," they said.
"It looks good on you."

The next morning Elmo stared at his breakfast gloomily. He was so worried about the day ahead that he forgot to tell his parents about his visit to Moogie. Leon was still asleep.

When the doorbell rang, Elmo got up sadly. "Now the trouble begins," he thought.

But when he opened the door he was amazed to see that Buford Snark was wearing a cap nearly as silly as his own. They stared at each other for a moment, then both began to laugh. "Mr. Kleeg?" asked Elmo, and Buford nodded.

It was a warm, sunny morning
in the city as the boys headed
off to school.
While they walked
they talked about summer,
and movies, and nearly
anything else they could think of,
except haircuts.

For
Mom and
Dad

ISBN 0-590-43331-8

Copyright © 1990 by Mark Teague.
All rights reserved. Published by Scholastic Inc.

BLUE RIBBON is a registered trademark of Scholastic Inc.

12 11 10 9 8 7 6 5 4 3 2   2 3 4 5 6/9
Printed in the U.S.A.   08